Copyright © 2002 by Michael Neugebauer Verlag, an imprint of
Nord-Süd Verlag AG, Gossau Zürich, Switzerland
First published in Switzerland under the title *Willibald, der Weihnachtsbaum*
English translation copyright © 2003 by North-South Books Inc., New York

First published in the United States, Great Britain, Canada, Australia, and
New Zealand in 2003 by North-South Books, an imprint of Nord-Süd Verlag AG,
Gossau Zürich, Switzerland.

Distributed in the United States by North-South Books Inc., New York.

Library of Congress Cataloging-in-Publication Data is available.
A CIP catalogue record for this book is available from The British Library.
ISBN 0-7358-1760-X (trade edition) 10 9 8 7 6 5 4 3 2 1
ISBN 0-7358-1761-8 (library edition) 10 9 8 7 6 5 4 3 2 1
Printed in Italy

For more information about our books, and the authors and artists
who create them, visit our web site: www.northsouth.com

THE LITTLE CHRISTMAS TREE

By **KARL RÜHMANN**

Illustrated by **ANNE MÖLLER**

Translated by J. ALISON JAMES

A MICHAEL NEUGEBAUER BOOK

NORTH-SOUTH BOOKS

New York · London

ONCE there was a fir tree that grew at the edge of the forest. Behind it, the great pines towered, and an oak tree spread its shadow far and wide. Birds built their nests in the pines; squirrels ate the nuts and acorns. Children had even built a tree house in the oak. But nobody, not even a mouse, thought the fir tree was useful. It was just too little. The little tree hated being so small. It felt as if nobody took it seriously. Some day I'll show them, the fir tree thought. But it didn't know how.

One day two hares came over the meadow to the edge of the forest. "Hey, take a look at that," cried one, pointing to the fir tree. "We can use that for jumping practice. It is just the right size."

The hare got a running start and took a great leap, right over the fir tree.
The second hare did the same.
The little tree was green with anger. But no matter how high it stretched, it couldn't even reach the hair on their bellies with its needles. Just you wait, it thought. Someday I'll show you. It just didn't know how.

Another time, a hedgehog came by. She was in a terrible mood. She'd been rummaging through the nearby houses' compost pile, and now her spines were all messy, covered in potato peelings, bread crusts, even a salami wrapper.

When she saw the fir tree she exclaimed, "Oh my! That tiny little tree is just the right size!" And before the fir tree could pull back its needles, the hedgehog scooted in among its branches and scraped off all the muck.

The fir tree trembled with fury. Just you wait! it thought, wobbling its tender green tip. Someday all of you will see what I can do! But it still didn't know how.

In autumn, the air grew chilly. A cold wind blew down the branches and stripped the leaves from their trees. Only conifers, like the pines and the fir tree, stayed green. The animals were out enjoying the last of the sunshine before snow covered the fields.

And then came winter. Snow fell for three days. The little tree stood mournfully at the edge of the meadow. Every once in a while it would shiver the snow from its branches so it didn't completely disappear in a drift.

One bright morning the little tree heard the *crunch, crunch* of
footsteps. It was a boy named Peter and his father. They were looking
for the perfect tree to cut down and take home for Christmas.
Peter ran up to the fir tree. "This one!" he cried.
"This one here? It's so small," his father said.
"Not for me! For me it's just the right size," said Peter.
His father laughed out loud. "You're right. It *is* beautiful. And it is
exactly your size. But it would be a shame to cut it down when it is still
so young." He thought for a moment. "I know. What if we brought
decorations out here to the forest? We wouldn't have to cut the tree,
and it could keep growing as you keep growing. Every year it could
be your own wild Christmas tree, the same size as you."
"Oh, yes!" cried Peter.

That very afternoon Peter came back to the forest with his parents. They pulled a sled with a big box on it. From the box they took wonderful red and deep blue glass balls and hung them on the fir tree's branches. The tree took great care not to drop a single ball. There wasn't enough room for all the balls, so Peter set the rest in a ring around the base of the tree.

Finally Peter fastened a gold star on the top. The star was quite heavy, but the fir tree was so proud that it didn't bend a bit.

"Wonderful," said the father.

"Really just the perfect size for you," said the mother.

"It's the most beautiful Christmas tree I've ever seen," Peter said.

The next day, all the animals came to see the little Christmas tree. They were awed by its beauty. The fir tree knew it had finally shown them that it was indeed just the right size—for something truly special.

Every year at Christmastime, Peter came back. Every year Peter and the fir tree grew a little bigger, but no matter how tall the tree grew— even when it towered over Peter's head—it stayed just the right size. And the fir tree remained the most beautiful Christmas tree for Peter his whole life long.